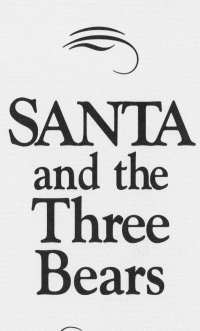

SANTA
and the
Three
Bears

SANTA
and the
Three Bears

Dominic Catalano

Boyds Mills Press

*Dedicated to
all the children
who bring the
magic and joy
to Christmas*

Text and illustrations copyright © 2000
by Dominic Catalano
All rights reserved

Published by Caroline House
Boyds Mills Press, Inc.
A Highlights Company
815 Church Street
Honesdale, Pennsylvania 18431
Printed in Hong Kong

U.S. Cataloging-in-Publication Data
   (Library of Congress Standards)

Catalano, Dominic.
     Santa and the three bears / written
and illustrated by Dominic Catalano. —
1st ed.
[32]p. : col. ill. ; cm.
Summary: Three bears have a lot of
explaining to do when they are caught
sleeping in Santa's house.
ISBN 1-56397-864-4
1. Bears — Fiction. 2. Santa Claus—
Fiction. I. Title.
   [E] 21 2000 AC   CIP
99-69853

First edition, 2000
The text of this book is set in
16-point Usherwood Medium.

Visit our Web site:
www.boydsmillspress.com

10 9 8 7 6 5 4 3 2 1

One winter's night,
a jolly man, dressed in red,
flew south into the starry sky.
A silver compass pointed the way.

oon after he left, the jolly man's wife bundled up in her favorite woolen coat and called for her three helpers.

"Everything's ready for my husband's surprise party," she said. "But we need a tree to decorate!"

"We'll bring the sled," her helpers said.

In their hurry, they left the front door slightly ajar.

Close by, three bears pushed against the wind. The snow crunched under their feet.
"Where are we?" bellowed Papa Bear.
"My paws are frozen!" growled Mama Bear.
"I'm tired," whined Baby Bear.

They came upon a house nestled in the pines. Its
windows glowed with the light of a crackling fire.
   "A chance to get my bearings," sighed Papa Bear.
   "A place to warm my paws," purred Mama Bear.
   "Somebody carry me!" pleaded Baby Bear.

*T*hey huddled by the door and sniffed and sniffed.

"Careful now," warned Papa Bear.

"Just a peek," whispered Mama Bear.

"Something smells good," cried Baby Bear.

Suddenly, the door swung open. And this is what they saw. . . .

Twinkling lights and velvet stockings hung just right.
    A map of the world, dotted with pins, draped with a garland of holly and berries.
    A big table, piled high with cookies and cakes and salads and fruit and a bowl of punch.

"How fascinating," said Papa Bear, tearing away the garland to study the map.

"How homey," said Mama Bear, slipping on the stockings and draping the colored lights around her shoulders.

"How tasty!" said Baby Bear, stuffing himself with cookies and cakes.

The three bears went into the workshop.

"Wow!" shouted Papa Bear, turning on the conveyor belt.

"I love crafts!" exclaimed Mama Bear, squirting a bottle of glue.

"Watch me paint!" whooped Baby Bear as he sent red, blue, and yellow paint flying in the air.

In the den, they found a great big chair,
a medium-size chair, and three small chairs.

"Soft," sighed Papa Bear, sinking into the big chair.

"Comfy," purred Mama Bear, easing into the
middle-size chair.

"Too small!" whined Baby Bear, breaking the
last of the three small chairs.

$\mathcal{U}$pstairs, the three bears found a soft bed and crawled under the covers.

"Time for a snooze," yawned Papa Bear.

"Wake me for breakfast," murmured Mama Bear.

"Zzzzzzzzz," snored Baby Bear.

Just then, the jolly man's wife and her three helpers appeared at the open front door.

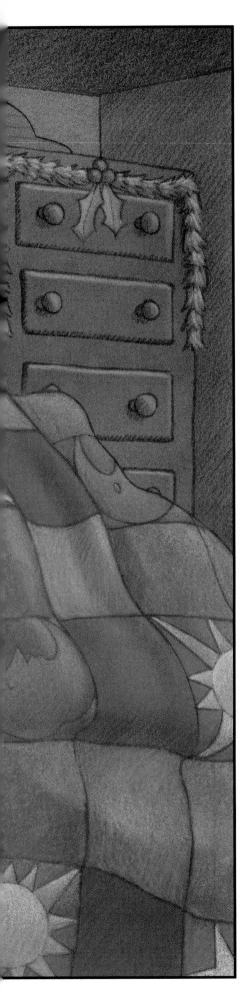

"Oh!" gasped the jolly man's wife. "Oh!" gasped her three helpers.

They went from room to room, shaking their heads. Finally, in the bedroom, they stopped and stared. There before their eyes were three sleeping bears.

"You!" said the jolly man's wife, taking Papa Bear by the ear.

She wagged her finger at Mama Bear and Baby Bear. "You all have a lot of work to do!"

The three bears helped make more cookies and cakes.
They rehung the stockings and garland and lights.
They swept and cleaned the workshop.
They straightened the den.
Finally, they trimmed the tree just right.
"A job well done," said the jolly man's wife.
"And just in time, too!"

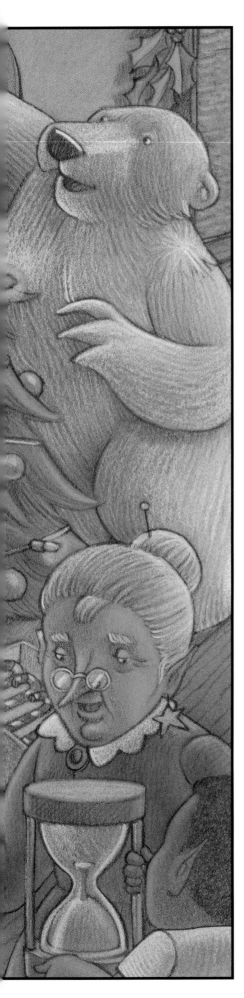
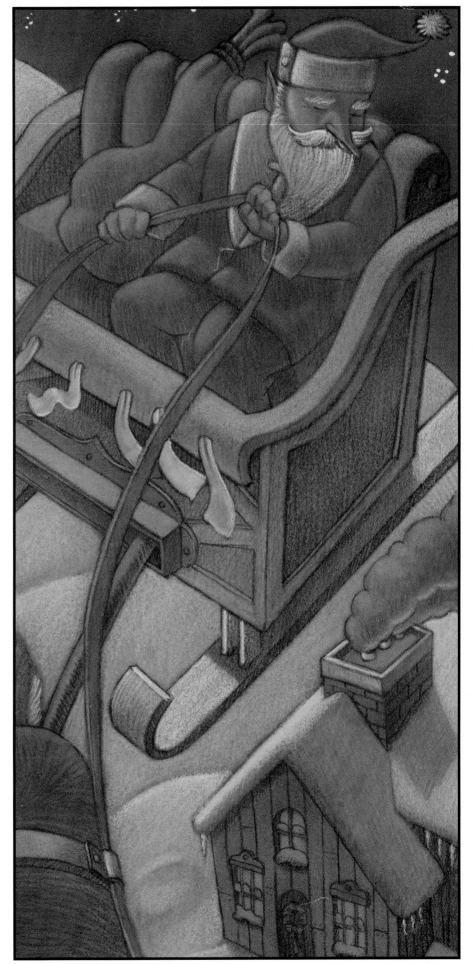

At that moment, the jolly man
came through the door.
    "Surprise!" they shouted.
    "Ho, ho, ho!" laughed the jolly man.
And what a Christmas party they had!

Everyone had lots of fun and opened lots of presents, but there were no presents for the three bears.

The jolly man frowned as he dug down deep in his bag.

"Empty," he said. "But the best gift is a gift that is dear." The jolly man held out his silver compass.

"Now I'll never be lost again!" said Papa Bear.

The jolly man's wife offered her coat.

"Now I'll be nice and warm!" cried Mama Bear.

The helpers brought their sled.

"Now I can ride!" squealed Baby Bear.

"Thank you!" said the three bears.

"Here's to new friends," said the jolly man.
And everyone cheered, "Merry Christmas to all!"